Dear Parent:
Your child's love of reading starts here!

Every child learns to read in a different way and at his or her own speed. Some go back and forth between reading levels and read favorite books again and again. Others read through each level in order. You can help your young reader improve and become more confident by encouraging his or her own interests and abilities. From books your child reads with you to the first books he or she reads alone, there are I Can Read Books for every stage of reading:

SHARED READING
Basic language, word repetition, and whimsical illustrations, ideal for sharing with your emergent reader

BEGINNING READING
Short sentences, familiar words, and simple concepts for children eager to read on their own

READING WITH HELP
Engaging stories, longer sentences, and language play for developing readers

READING ALONE
Complex plots, challenging vocabulary, and high-interest topics for the independent reader

ADVANCED READING
Short paragraphs, chapters, and exciting themes for the perfect bridge to chapter books

I Can Read Books have introduced children to the joy of reading since 1957. Featuring award-winning authors and illustrators and a fabulous cast of beloved characters, I Can Read Books set the standard for beginning readers.

A lifetime of discovery begins with the magical words **"I Can Read!"**

Visit www.icanread.com for information
on enriching your child's reading experience.

Pinkalicious™
The Pinkerrific Playdate

For Eileen and Esa!

XOX,

V.K.

The author gratefully acknowledges
the artistic and editorial contributions
of Wendy Wax and Susan Hill.

I Can Read Book® is a trademark of HarperCollins Publishers.

Pinkalicious: The Pinkerrific Playdate
Copyright © 2011 by Victoria Kann, Inc.

PINKALICIOUS and all related logos and characters
are trademarks of Victoria Kann, Inc. Used with permission.

Based on the HarperCollins book *Pinkalicious* written by
Victoria Kann and Elizabeth Kann, illustrated by Victoria Kann
All rights reserved. Printed in the United States of America.
No part of this book may be used or reproduced in any manner whatsoever without
written permission except in the case of brief quotations embodied in critical articles and reviews.
For information address HarperCollins Children's Books, a division of HarperCollins Publishers,
10 East 53rd Street, New York, NY 10022.
www.icanread.com

Library of Congress catalog card number: 2011929315
ISBN 978-0-06-192884-0 (trade bdg.) —ISBN 978-0-06-192883-3 (pbk.)

11 12 13 14 15 LP/WOR 10 9 8 7 6 5 4 3 2 1
❖
First Edition

Pinkalicious™
The Pinkerrific Playdate

by Victoria Kann

HARPER
An Imprint of HarperCollinsPublishers

I have a new friend.

Her name is Rose.

The wonderful thing about Rose

is that we have a great time

playing together.

Last week,

I didn't even know Rose's name.

All I knew about Rose

was that she was new at our school.

On Thursday, Alison said,

"Let's jump with both ropes."

"We can't," I said.

"We need three people for that."

"What about the new girl,
Rose?" Alison asked.

"What a beautiful name," I said.

"Let's ask her to play, too."

Rose could really jump!

Rose sat with us at lunch.

I shared my pink cupcakes.

Alison shared her beet salad.

Rose shared her strawberry smoothie.

Sharing is wonderful.

So is Rose!

Today, Alison has soccer.

Rose is coming over for a playdate
for the first time ever.

I can hardly wait!

dominoes ↗

cartwheels

make friendship bracelets

hula hoops

tea party with Dolly and Rabbit

"What are you going to do together?" asked Peter.

"It's all planned," I said.

"Is it time yet?" I asked Mommy.

"I'm so excited.

I can't wait!"

"Rose will have a wonderful time.

You've planned so much to do!"

said Mommy.

"This will be fun!" said Peter.

"You're not exactly invited," I said.

"Don't forget to include Peter, Pinkalicious," said Mommy.

Just then, the doorbell rang.

It was Rose!

"Come on, Rose," I said.

"Let's make friendship bracelets!"

"I like the colors you picked,"

said Rose.

"I like your colors, too," I told her.

"Look at me!

I'm playing, too," said Peter.

"It's time to bake cookies," I said.

"Pink sprinkles go on top!"

"Yummy!" said Rose.

"Fumfy," said Peter.

His mouth was full.

"Now it's hula hoop time!" I said.

Rose and I ran outside.

Peter came, too.

"I can hula two hoops!" said Rose.

"Me, too!" I said.

We talked about our favorite books.

We talked about our best birthdays so far.

We talked about our teacher
and the ice-skating rink.

We talked a lot.

Then we giggled about
our little brothers.
Rose has one, too!
I forgot all about my list
of things to do.

"Time to go," Rose's mom said.

"What?" Rose said.

"We didn't get to play dress-up,

or do the obstacle course,

or do the limbo," I wailed.

"I love to do the limbo,"

Rose said.

"Can we do that next time?"

She smiled at me.

I smiled back.

Peter smiled, too.

"This was the best playdate ever!"

he said.

"I think so, too, Peter!"

Rose said.

I smiled.

"Me, too!"